The Owls of Blossom Wood

First published in the UK in 2015 by Scholastic Children's Books

An imprint of Scholastic Ltd
Euston House, 24 Eversholt Street
London, NW1 1DB, UK
Registered office: Westfield Road, Southam, Warwickshire, CV47 0RA
SCHOLASTIC and associated logos are trademarks and/or registered
trademarks of Scholastic Inc.

Text copyright © Catherine Coe, 2015
Cover copyright © Andrew Farley represented by Meiklejohn, 2015
Inside illustration copyright © Renée Kurilla, 2015

The rights of Catherine Coe and Renée Kurilla to be identified as the
author and illustrator of this work have been asserted by them.

ISBN 978 1407 15665 1

A CIP catalogue record for this book is available from the British Library

Printed and bound by CPI Group (UK) Ltd, Croydon, CR0 4YY
Papers used by Scholastic Children's Books are made from wood
grown in sustainable forests.

1 3 5 7 9 10 8 6 4 2

This is a work of fiction. Names, characters, places, incidents and
dialogue are products of the author's imagination or are used
fictitiously.

The Owls of Blossom Wood

Lost and Found

Catherine Coe

SCHOLASTIC

For Molly Challis,
with lots of love xxx

Chapter 1
The Fete

Katie shook out her great white wings. "We're owls again!" Moments earlier, she'd been a blonde-haired girl — now she was an elegant snowy owl!

Eva, now a barn owl, swivelled her pretty, heart-shaped face around, taking in the beautiful woodland surrounding them. "And we're back in Blossom Wood!"

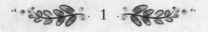

Alex, a little owl and the smallest of the three, hopped along the branch of the Moon Chestnut tree, ruffling her brown feathers. "And it's gorgeous!" It was as if someone had scattered tons of pretty confetti all over the wood – for the trees were coated in blossom, as far as their eyes could see. Yellow, pink, purple, red, blue, lilac. It was an incredible sight!

The three best friends had, just minutes before, been girls in Katie's garden. Then they'd found the special white feather inside the hollow chestnut tree trunk. It had magically transported them to the Moon Chestnut tree in the middle of Blossom Wood, and changed them into owls once again!

"Look, there's Bobby!" Katie leapt off the high branch and soared towards the badger on the ground. Her huge wings swooped in the still spring air and her talons tingled with the excitement of flying again.

Eva went next, spreading her light-brown wings to float slowly to the ground. It felt fantastic to be able to flutter in the air once more.

Alex was the last owl to jump from the tree. She flapped her little wings quickly, darting between the branches and grinning with happiness.

"Hello, dearest owls," said Bobby, beaming.

Alex landed with a rustle on the blossom-covered ground, and smiled back.

"Hi, Bobby," said Eva, stroking the petals on the floor with her wingtips. "It's SO pretty in the wood right now. I mean, not that it isn't always pretty, of course!"

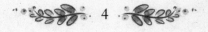

Katie turned her head almost all the
way round — first to the left, then to the
right, looking for clues. The badger left
the feather out for them when there was
a problem in the wood and he needed
their help. "So, Bobby, what's the matter?

Bobby's grin stretched even wider
across his stripy face. "Ah, now, my

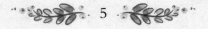

wonderful owl friends, I very much hope
you don't mind …" he began in his
gravelly voice.

Eva tilted her head to one side. What
was he going to say?

"… but I thought you might like to
attend our springtime fete today!"

"Don't *mind*?" hooted Katie. "That
sounds brilliant!"

Bobby clapped his black leathery paws
together. "Oh, that's marvellous! You see,

it's such an extra-special time in Blossom Wood that we really didn't want you to miss it."

"I can see that." Alex spun her fluffy little head round to look up at the trees. "It's beautiful!"

But Eva was frowning. "It's spring here? That's weird – at home, it's autumn, and cold and—" Eva stopped when she realized Katie and Alex were staring at her. Then she remembered – Bobby didn't know they were from a completely different place, where they were not owls, but girls.

Alex quickly changed the subject. "Can we help with anything for the fete?"

Bobby's black eyes twinkled. "Oh, you owls are so generous. I'm sure there are woodlanders who'd love some assistance. Perhaps you could help the caterpillars

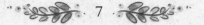

put up the silk bunting they've made? They're having trouble hanging it…"

"Oh, yes, please – could you help, owls?" Wilf the caterpillar's tiny voice floated across from a nearby hedgerow.

They looked over. Hundreds of ants carried beautiful silvery silk bunting on their backs while bright-green caterpillars held it at the ends, jumping up and trying to hook it on to the hedge. Every time, it came floating back down.

"No problem!" Katie hopped over to the ants and caterpillars and took one end in her little black beak. Eva rushed over to hold the other end, and they flew up to the top of the hedge and hung it neatly, tying each end around a branch to secure it.

"There!" said Eva, clapping her wings at a job well done.

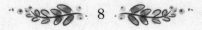

Meanwhile, Alex had spotted a group
of honeybees trying to carry something
down from the Moon Chestnut tree.
She flapped her small brown wings and
zoomed up towards them. "Can I help?"
she asked shyly.

Bella, a bee they'd met the first time
they'd visited Blossom Wood, peeped out
from behind a large straw basket. Alex

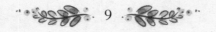

knew that Bella was even more timid than she was.

More than twenty bees were trying to lift the basket from the branch where it balanced, but it toppled about, not looking very safe *at all*. "Oh, Alex, that would be really kind – thank you," Bella buzzed.

Alex moved up until she was hovering above the branch and ever so slowly clutched the basket handle in her talons. Making sure she gripped it tightly, she fluttered her wings and glided gently to the ground, the bees buzzing along behind her. As she flew, the most amazing honey smell wafted out. *Yummmmm.*

"What's inside?" Alex asked as she nestled the basket carefully on the ground.

"Honey cookies!" the bees replied.

"Honeycomb!"

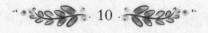

"Honey jelly!"

"And honey juice!"

Bella flew up to Alex's ear. "Don't forget, you can have as much honey as you want," she whispered. Bella had promised the owls unlimited honey after

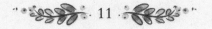

they'd helped save the Moon Chestnut tree. It was the most important tree in the wood, because it was the oldest, and everyone believed it was magical. It had been brown and droopy and dying the first time they'd been here – but now it was healthy and full of life.

Alex grinned at the thought of delicious honey jelly. "I'll make sure I come and find you at the fete!"

Just as the three best friends were gathering back together, a little black furry ball rushed past. "Is that who I think it is?" Katie asked in surprise.

Eva blinked. "Pete?!" The mole hated leaving his home, so it was very strange to see him running around like this. They'd had to persuade him to move house quite recently, when they'd realized it was Pete's tunnelling around the Moon

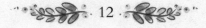

Chestnut tree's roots that had made it ill.

Bobby, who'd been organizing the fireflies into lights for the fete, nodded. "He seems to have turned over a new leaf, at least for today's fete – he's going to open up his home for the rest of the woodlanders to enjoy!" To encourage Pete to move, the rabbits had built him an exciting new place to live, with roller-coaster tunnels, slides and all sorts. Really,

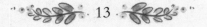

it was more like a theme park than a home!

"I wish we had something we could donate to the fete, too," hooted Alex.

Eva sighed. "Oh yes, the rose-petal necklaces I made last week would've been perfect!"

"Hang on." Katie's orange eyes glistened as an idea popped into her head. "Could we go home to get them?"

"I'm not sure … would we be able to come back right away?" Alex worried.

"Absolutely!" said Bobby. "I'll leave the feather out just as soon as you're gone. Then, once you've got the necklaces – which sound delightful, by the way – you'll be able to return immediately!"

"That's sorted, then!" Katie was already soaring up to the branch of the Moon Chestnut tree that would magically take them home.

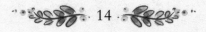

Eva and Alex fluttered into the sky behind Katie. As the three best friends landed at the top of the tree, they smiled down at the busy woodlanders darting about the forest. Happy chatter floated up into the air from all around.

They waved to Bobby, calling out, "See you soon!"

Chapter 2
Girls Again

The three best friends stood together on the upper branch of the tree and held wingtips. They clamped their eyes shut, waiting for what would happen next. Sure enough, it wasn't long before they were whizzing and spinning, as if they were caught up in a hurricane. Wind buffeted them all about as they spun around

crazily, not daring to open their eyes, but they kept hold of each other tightly and waited for the spinning to stop.

As it began to slow down, they finally looked around. All they could see now was tree bark, because they were back inside the hollow fallen tree trunk in Katie's garden, girls once more!

Katie put her hands through her long blonde hair and her blue eyes sparkled. "That was brilliant!"

Eva nodded. She had bobbed brown hair and green eyes. "Owls one minute, girls the next!"

Alex, the shortest of the three girls, with black curly hair and brown eyes, crawled out of the tree trunk. She didn't like all the spinning so much, but it was worth it to be able to transform into owls and back again!

"OK, you go and get the necklaces, Eva," said Katie, scrambling out on her knees.

Eva jumped out of the trunk behind Katie. She put her hand to her head and did a fake salute. "Yes, sir!"

Katie felt her cheeks rush with blood. "Oh, sorry – I didn't mean to be bossy!"

Eva winked at her friend. Katie could be a little bossy, but Eva didn't mind really. "It's all right – I know you just

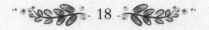

want to get back to Blossom Wood as quickly as possible!"

The girls could go to Blossom Wood only when the white feather was left inside the tree trunk for them. It had seemed like for ever since the last time they'd visited (though in actual fact it had been just a week). The three best friends would have loved to visit Blossom Wood every day if they could, it was so amazing.

Alex bit her lip. "I want to go and get something too," she said quietly. She sprinted up the garden path and turned left out of the gate to her bungalow next door.

Behind her, Eva turned right – she lived the other side of Katie's ivy-covered house, in a thatched cottage.

With her friends gone, Katie ran inside

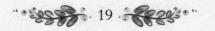

through the back door, waved to her mum sitting at the kitchen table behind her laptop, and leapt up the stairs two at a time. She'd thought of something that might make the fete extra special.

A minute later, Katie rushed back into the kitchen with reams of thick ribbon in her hands, in all the colours of the rainbow. "Mum, can I borrow these? I'll put them back in the sewing cupboard later, I promise."

Her mum looked up from her screen. "Yes, OK – as long as you return them!" She went back to her writing and Katie ran into the garden, stuffing the ribbons into her jeans pockets.

Eva and Alex were already waiting among the wildflowers around the trunk at the bottom of Katie's garden.

"You were quick!" Katie said breathlessly.

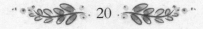

"Where did you go? We thought you might have been caught by Alfie." Eva looked behind Katie as if her younger brother might jump out at any second.

Katie grinned a wide smile. "He's at his swimming lesson this morning, thank treetops. I ran inside to get something for the fete too!"

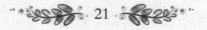

Alex laughed. "Thank treetops" was one of Bobby's sayings. She ducked her head into the trunk. "Phew – it's there." The glossy white feather lay in the middle of the dark trunk. She shuffled in first, and sat down at the far end. Inside, the trunk always seemed even bigger than from outside – Alex didn't even catch her big hair on the roof. She tucked her donation to the fete – a collage she'd made the previous week using her favourite leaves from the garden – under her arm. She thought it might be a nice prize for the raffle. *But maybe they're fed up with leaves*, she suddenly worried. *It could be the last thing a woodlander would want on their wall!*

But there was no time to change her mind. Eva grabbed Alex's and Katie's hands. Alex plucked up the feather and shut her eyes tight. The familiar

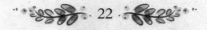

whooshing noise began, a whistling wind
pushed past their ears, and they spun and
spun and spun.

It seemed to be taking ages, Eva
was thinking, when at last she felt the
movement start to slow. Her toes tingled
and fingers fizzed reassuringly. Sure
enough, when she flashed her eyes open,
she was back as an owl, teetering high on

a tree branch, the blossom-covered wood spread out before her.

Katie flapped her wings. "Blossom Wood fete, here we come!"

"Wait — something's wrong," twittered Alex. She had the feeling that something was different, although she couldn't work out quite what.

Katie bounced along the Moon Chestnut branch, her ribbons gripped in her talons. "What do you mean?"

Alex bobbed her head, then frowned as she realized what the difference was. "When we were here earlier, there was a lot of happy chattering with everyone getting ready for the fete. Listen to how quiet it is now..."

All three stood still on the branch, not moving a feather. The only sound they could hear was the rustling of the trees.

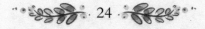

"Let's go and investigate." Katie jumped off the branch and swooped to the ground. Eva and Alex fluttered behind her graceful snowy-white shape, holding the necklaces and the collage in their beaks. At the base of the chestnut tree, many different creatures of the wood – frogs and mice and foxes and squirrels – were rushing about. But no one was talking, and many had deep frowns on their faces.

"Excuse me!" Eva called to a passing hedgehog. "What's happening? Is everything OK?"

The hedgehog turned her prickly head to them. "Not really," she began in her high-pitched, staccato voice. You'd better go and see Bobby. He's at home, I think!" And she scampered away.

"Oh dear." Alex hopped anxiously from leg to leg. "I wonder what's the matter?

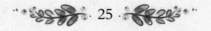

Quick, let's find Bobby's sett!"

As bubbles of worry rose in their chests, the three best friends took running jumps and flew off together into the bright blue sky.

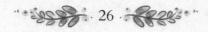

Chapter 3
Oh Deer

Alex, Katie and Eva had never been to Bobby's home before, but they remembered he'd mentioned it was near the edge of the Oval of Oaks.

With their gifts for the fete held tightly in their talons, they soared upwards, using their fantastic owl eyesight to scan the thick green trees below them. Here, more

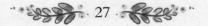

animals ran about frantically, just as they'd seen back at the Moon Chestnut. What was going on?

In the gap between the Oval of Oaks and Echo Mountains, Alex spotted mounds of brown earth with some badger-size holes dotted about. Together these looked just like the kind of badger home she'd seen in nature documentaries!

"Could that be it?" Alex tipped her head down, swooping lower to get a closer look.

"Let's go and see!" Katie hooted.

They dipped their wings first left, then right, to fly slowly downwards, taking care to avoid the branches of the oak trees. When they were a few metres from the ground, they could hear a medley of bleating noises coming from one of the

holes. *Is that Bobby?* wondered Eva. *It doesn't sound like his deep voice...*

The three friends landed round the hole and Alex, being the smallest owl, poked her head inside. "Hello?" she said into the darkness. In the distance she spotted a black-and-white-striped blur. Bobby!

"Oh, owls, how glad I am to see you! Please, do come in!"

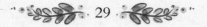

Alex beckoned Eva and Katie with a wing, then hopped in first. She could fit inside the burrow easily, but she guessed it would be a squeeze for Eva, who was double her size, and even harder for Katie, the largest of the owls.

Alex was right. At the back, Katie had to duck her snowy head and shuffle along, her wings tight against the burrow's walls. But after a few moments, the tunnel opened out into a large, homely room, decorated with woven-grass rugs and moth-silk wall hangings. It was lit with pretty beeswax tealights all around the edge. As Katie stretched out her wings, she saw Bobby surrounded by balls of brown fur. When she looked closer, she realized the fluffy balls were young deer!

Bobby's head poked out between the fawns who climbed over him. "I'm

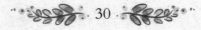

30

babysitting," he explained. "Come on, children, now – off you get."

Eva giggled. Bobby might have been babysitting, but really it was the fawns who were doing the sitting – on him! As far as she knew, the kind old badger hadn't any children of his own, and it didn't look as if he knew quite what to do with them. Luckily, with a baby sister at home, Eva did. "Hey, kids," she called, clapping her wings together, "let's go outside!"

The cute fawns all turned their chestnut-coloured heads to Eva and scampered over. She led them out of Bobby's home, still clapping her wings.

She looks like the Pied Piper! thought Alex with a grin.

Bobby brushed himself down. "They're lovely children, but rather a handful!"

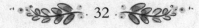

"So why are you babysitting them?"
asked Katie.

Bobby's smile vanished. "I'm afraid
there's a terrible reason: Flo, the youngest
fawn, has gone missing!"

Alex put a wing to her beak in horror.
"Oh no! We saw everyone rushing about
when we got back to Blossom Wood –
are they all looking for her?"

"Yes, yes – all the woodland creatures are helping her mother, Sara, to search for Flo. My legs aren't what they once were, I'm sorry to say, so I volunteered to look after Sara's other children. But so far they haven't found her. Poor Sara is very upset, of course. She'd left their home beside Foxglove Glade to collect apples for her tart for the fete, and she was only gone for a few minutes. But when she returned, Flo had disappeared."

Bobby gave a big sniff and shook his head sadly. Alex laid a wing on his paw. She'd never seen the badger so upset before.

Katie put her snowy head to one side, confused. "But how could Flo have gone anywhere if she's just a baby?"

"I think baby deer start to walk when they're really young. Is that right, Bobby?"

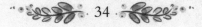

Alex asked the badger.

Bobby nodded. "Yes, deer can gallop about within a few hours of being born. Flo's a few days old. She hasn't even been blessed at the Moon Chestnut tree yet."

Since everyone believed the tree was magical, every baby born in the wood was taken to the Moon Chestnut to be blessed with wishes for a long life.

Eva hopped back into Bobby's living room just then. "I made the fawns a skipping-rope out of grasses – that should keep them busy for a while." She looked round at everyone's downturned mouths. "What's happened?"

Katie explained what Bobby had just told them. "We've got to find Flo – she's only little!" she finished.

Eva felt sick with worry. She imagined how terrible she'd feel if her baby sister

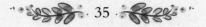

went missing – and how upset her parents would be. She was thankful that Belle could only crawl at the moment. She couldn't escape so easily!

"We should join the search party right away!" Alex was already flapping towards the exit of the sett. "Bobby, will you be all right by yourself, with the fawns?"

"Yes, yes, you must go," said Bobby in his deep voice. "Thank treetops you're here! With your wings and your wonderful eyesight, you'll be able to cover an awful lot of ground. I'll manage with the little ones. Somehow!"

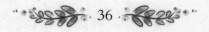

Chapter 4
The Search

Alex stared and stared and stared some more. As she flew above Blossom Wood, she didn't even blink, she was looking so hard. They'd started searching as soon as they'd said goodbye to Bobby and the fawns, leaving their things for the fete behind in Bobby's sett. *We have to find Flo — we just* have *to!* Alex thought.

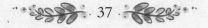

Eva was so focused on the ground that she almost flew into Katie. "Sorry!" she cried as she grazed Katie's tail with her wingtip, then tipped herself to the right to avoid a full-on collision.

Katie smiled at her clumsy friend. She was so confident at flying now that the brush with Eva hadn't upset her rhythm at all. "Don't worry!"

The three best friends kept going. They passed the Oval of Oaks and the Moon Chestnut tree, scanning the ground for any sign of a baby deer. They soared over Pine Forest, swooping between the dark-green pointy treetops, but they couldn't see Flo there either.

Alex slowed down, feeling frustrated. "How will we ever find her?"

Eva sighed. "I don't know — she could be anywhere!"

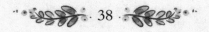

Katie turned back to her friends.
"Come on — we can't give up." She
flapped her wings harder than ever.
"We've got so much more of Blossom
Wood to check!" She zoomed away,
beckoning Eva and Alex to follow.

Eva felt glad to have such a
determined friend. *And Flo* has *to be
somewhere*, she thought, as they continued
onwards. The pretty Apple Orchard stretched
out beneath them like a polka-dot blanket,

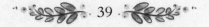

filled with apple trees laden with fruit.

The three best friends could still
see lots of animals racing about below,
looking for Flo – squirrels, mice, rabbits,
even caterpillars and worms. In the sky
around them, birds soared, their eyes
fixed downwards, scanning the ground.
Charles, a blackbird and the Blossom
Wood singing teacher, flew over to Katie.
The friends had first met him when he'd
tried to teach them to sing – though
the lessons hadn't been very successful,
unfortunately! Back then, they'd been
scared of the grumpy blackbird, but they'd
soon realized that, as Bobby had reassured
them, his twit was much worse than
his tweet.

"Have you owls seen any sign of Flo?"
his deep, posh voice echoed in the wind.

Katie grimaced. "No, I'm afraid not.

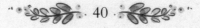

But we won't give up!"

"That's the spirit," Charles replied. "I
do hope we can return Flo to her mother
safely." He tilted his glossy black head
down. "I'm going to search closer to the
Great Hedge. Good luck, owls."

They waved goodbye without taking
their eyes off the woodland floor. They
were reaching the end of Apple Orchard,
near to a large patch of brown ground.
This was the Brown Desert, where only
Pete lived.

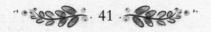

All of a sudden, Alex spun round to her friends. "What about the Brown Desert? That's where we first met Sara — she told us the deer often exercise there. Maybe that's where Flo went to?"

"Good thinking, Alex!" Eva felt a bubble of hope float up inside her. Perhaps no one had thought of checking there. They zoomed off to the Brown Desert and began scouring the muddy, grassless land.

Although the ground was a very similar colour to Flo, with their excellent owl eyesight they'd still be able to spot her if she was there. But as they swooped back and forth, north to south, south to north, there was absolutely no sign of the baby deer anywhere.

Alex breathed heavily. She'd started to feel tired, which wasn't surprising since

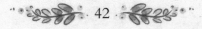

her little wings needed a lot more flapping
to fly the same distance as her friends. But
she didn't want to complain – she didn't
want to let anyone down. So she was glad
when Eva said, "Do you think we could
stop for a rest? Perhaps we can go back
to the Moon Chestnut tree and see how
everyone else is getting on."

Katie nodded her snowy-white head.
"Good idea. We can find out which
places are still left to search – and maybe
someone has found Flo, and we just don't
know it yet!"

The three best friends turned in the
direction of the Moon Chestnut tree.
Alex noticed that the sky had darkened,
and grey storm clouds were moving in.
As they flew, the clouds thickened and
turned inky-blue, as if they might burst at
any minute.

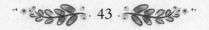

They landed at the base of the crescent-moon-shaped tree, where they found a couple of red foxes scowling at three beavers.

"You live close to the deer," one of the foxes was saying. "You should've found her by now!"

Eva saw his white-tipped tail and realized he was the fox they'd helped cure of fleas on their last visit to Blossom Wood.

"Did you really look ALL around Foxglove Glade, or have I gotta do it for you?" he continued.

"Yes, yes, yes!" squealed a toothy beaver. "But if you don't believe me, then go and check for yourself, smelly!"

"Oi, Jonny, who are you calling smelly?" The other fox held up his front paws as if preparing for a fight.

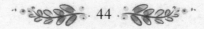

Katie flung out one huge wing
between the animals. "Hey, hey, hey,
please don't fight — that won't help us
get Flo back!"

The foxes and the beavers all took a
step backwards and hung their heads.

"Sorry," said Jonny, his voice still high
but now very quiet. "We just don't know

what to do — we can't find little Flo anywhere."

"And now it's raining!" twittered Eva. She looked up at the gloomy clouds as raindrops began pattering on her glossy feathers. The gorgeous silvery bunting for the fete drooped sadly in the rain.

All the animals nearby huddled closer to the Moon Chestnut tree, sheltering under its outstretched branches. The squirrels flopped their tails over their backs and heads to keep them dry, like their very own attached umbrellas!

Alex looked out at the big raindrops, which made *plink plonk* sounds on the leaves. Normally she would have enjoyed being right in the middle of all this wildlife — and she loved splashing in the rain — but all she could think about was poor Flo, all alone, getting terribly wet.

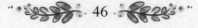

"Flo will be soaked!" said Katie as
the raindrops bounced even harder all
around them.

"Oh, you don't need to worry about
that!" came a familiar voice. One of their
friends, a wren named Winnie, fluttered
down from the branch above. "Flo won't
care a diddly-squat about the rain – deer
love the water and swimming!"

"Swimming? Really?" Alex's little fluffy

eyebrows stretched high up her head. She thought she knew a lot about nature and animals, but she'd never heard of deer swimming before!

"We didn't even think of checking Willow Lake!" hooted Eva. "Has anyone?"

All the creatures around them shook their heads.

Katie put a wing to her forehead. "Maybe Flo has been there all along!"

"Come on, let's go and look!" Not caring how wet her feathers might get, Alex hopped away from the shelter of the chestnut tree.

Her two best friends were right behind her. They ran along the muddy ground, fluttered their wings as best they could in the rain and took off into the showery sky.

Chapter 5
The Rescue

The woodland below looked a lot different from before, now that most of the creatures were hiding from the rain. Only the worms were visible, slithering across the floor of Apple Orchard, as if they enjoyed getting wet!

Katie had to keep blinking her eyes as they fluttered through the pouring

rain. They'd never tried flying in such weather before and it was much harder — because their wings got wet and heavy very quickly. But it didn't stop them — they had to get to Willow Lake. Katie could see it in the distance, beyond Apple Orchard. It wasn't sparkling as it usually did, but instead was dimpled all over from the falling raindrops.

Eva dipped her head and began to descend towards the silvery willow trees surrounding the lake. Their long leaves drooped low, dripping raindrops like hundreds of dribbling taps. Eva landed by a tree and stepped through the wet curtain of willow leaves — and saw the lake filled with toads of all colours and sizes, bouncing up and down on the lily pads. It looked as if these creatures liked the rain too!

Katie stepped out behind Eva. She

didn't want to spoil the toads' fun, but they had to keep searching for Flo. "Excuse me," she said to the nearest toad — a small red speckled thing with big brown eyes. "Have you seen Flo the baby deer around here? We think she might be in the water somewhere."

"Oh, ribbity ribbit!" The toad jumped over to the shore of the lake and shook his wet, slimy head. "No, I'm sorry, ribbit. We haven't seen her here." He squelched sadly back to his lily pad.

"Oh no!" Alex, the last to arrive at the lake, bobbed her head in despair as she landed on the shore and heard the toad's reply. She'd really thought Flo would be there.

"What do we do now?" hooted Katie. The three best friends hopped backwards into the damp grass under a willow tree.

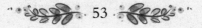

They stared at the lake, pitter-pattering with the steady rain.

After a few moments, Alex jumped up – startling her friends. "Hang on!" She fluttered to the edge of the water.

"Please be careful, Alex!" Katie called. "I'm pretty sure owls can't swim!"

Alex swivelled her head around. "Don't worry – I'm not going in. But I've noticed something. Come here!"

Katie and Eva rushed to join Alex. The little owl pointed a wingtip at the lake's edge, where the water lapped back and forth, back and forth.

"I think this lake is fed by a river – that's what makes the water move backwards and forwards like that. We've seen a river when we've been flying across Blossom Wood. Maybe Flo could be somewhere there – couldn't she?"

"Ribbit!" The toad they'd talked to earlier must have overheard, for he bounced back to the owls. "It's possible – but the Rushing River flows ribbitingly fast. It's very dangerous, ribbit! We didn't think of looking there because it's not a place for swimming…"

"But Flo might not know that," twittered Eva. "She's only a baby!"

Alex was already flapping her wings against the rain and flying up into the stormy sky. As she rose above the willow trees she could see how the lake connected to the river in one corner. She waited a moment for Eva and Katie to join her, and the three friends zoomed together towards the Rushing River so they could fly right above it. The river wasn't very wide – about the width of Katie's fully spread wings – so they flew in a row, Katie in the middle, her eyes peeled on the moving water, Alex on the left, checking one riverbank, and Eva on the right, searching the other. They fluttered along as slowly as they could, just a couple of metres above the water.

They passed the Brown Desert and Apple Orchard on either side. As the river began curling round the edge of Pine

Forest, Eva gasped. "I can see something – some brown fur!" She dipped lower, even closer to the riverbank.

Alex followed the gaze of her friend and spotted the patch of brown tucked into a hole at the very edge of the muddy bank. She tried not to get too excited, but she couldn't stop her wingtips tingling. Alex and Katie shot down behind Eva, who was hovering just

a few centimetres above the river now, the water splashing her talons as it swept past.

"Flo?" Eva tweeted gently, though she had to raise her voice to be heard over the sound of the rushing water.

Katie saw the brown fur move ever so slightly, revealing little white spots. She felt as if her heart had leapt right into her beak.

Alex fluttered closer, and ducked her head into the hole. It was Flo! She could see the little fawn shivering inside, and could hear a few distressed bleats. Alex held out a sodden wing. "Flo, it's OK. Come with us – we'll take you back to your mummy."

The baby fawn raised her chestnut head. She looked exactly like her brothers and sisters – only much smaller.

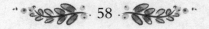

Her big brown eyes were wide with
fear, but she started to shuffle towards
Alex.

"That's right," the little owl continued
quietly. "Katie will fly down here to
us and you can ride on her back." She
beckoned to Katie, who nodded and

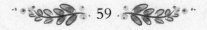

lowered herself by tilting her wings one way, then the other.

To reach the hole in the bank, Katie had to fly down so low that her belly was touching the river water. But she didn't mind getting even wetter if they could save the baby deer. Alex and Eva held out their wings and helped Flo on to Katie's back. The fawn collapsed into Katie's thick white feathers, and Katie fluffed them as much as possible to warm up the tiny deer.

"At least it isn't raining any more," said Eva, noticing that the raindrops had stopped as they flew extra slowly up into the sky.

Katie fluttered very carefully now she had Flo on her back. She certainly wouldn't perform any of her usual loop-the-loops or somersaults.

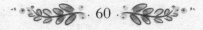

"Thank you," Alex heard Flo whisper as they travelled below the drifting clouds. Alex smiled at the baby deer, wondering what she'd been doing at the river. She decided that now probably wasn't the best time to ask.

"Here we are!" Katie said at last, as she tilted forward and carefully floated down to the deer's home at the edge of Foxglove Glade.

Sara, Flo's mother, must have spotted them from far away. She stood in the grasses, staring upwards, her mouth gaping open and her legs trembling. "Flo," she whispered. "Is that really you?"

The baby fawn was sensible enough not to move until Katie had landed on the ground a few metres away from Sara, near the glowing multicoloured foxgloves that surrounded the glade.

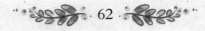

The mother deer galloped over – and Flo leapt from Katie's back. "Where have you been?" bleated Sara sternly, although the smile on her face showed she was more relieved than angry. "What in Blossom Wood did you think you were doing?" Sara bent her silky head down over her baby, cuddling her as they stood.

"We found her in a hole in the bank of the Rushing River," Katie said.

"Had you been trying to swim?" Alex asked Flo.

The young fawn nodded. "Everyone else talks about swimming – Joe and Daisy and Lucy and George. I wanted to try!"

Sara fixed Flo's eyes with hers. "But your brothers and sisters do that in Willow Lake, where it's safe! Not in the rapids of the river. If you'd asked to go, I would have explained that."

"At least she's safe now," said Eva, putting a wing on Sara's back. Eva felt so glad they'd found Flo, and couldn't be too angry at the young fawn – Flo hadn't realized how dangerous it would be, or that she'd get stuck.

"You're right," said Sara, pulling her

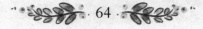

eyes away from Flo to look at the owls. "Thank you so, so, SO much for finding Flo and returning her safely to me." She bent back down to her youngest daughter. "Now, it's a warm bath for you, and some milk-thistle tea. My baby, I was so worried about you." Sara nuzzled Flo closer, cooing and bleating.

Just at that moment, the sun pushed out from behind the final cloud, bathing Blossom Wood in beautiful yellow light. Flo and Sara waved goodbye and trotted away.

Alex felt her eyes grow hot with happiness. A tear of joy brimmed over and dripped to the ground.

Eva smiled at the mother and baby deer as they left, then turned to her friends. "What should we do now?"

Katie spun a pirouette on her talons.

"The fete! Now that Flo has been found, it can go ahead!"

"Oh yes!" Alex clapped her wings together and looked to the sky. "And now we have the perfect weather for it!"

Chapter 6
A Magical End

The muddy ground meant it was not *quite* the perfect weather for the fete, but none of the woodlanders seemed to mind in the slightest. Not now that Flo was back home safely.

The three best friends had flown to Bobby's sett immediately and told him the good news. Katie, Alex and Eva had

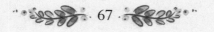

collected their things and rushed to the Moon Chestnut tree, leaving Bobby to bring Flo's brothers and sisters to the fete. Word spread quickly that Flo had been rescued and the fete would go ahead, and within minutes Blossom Wood was filled once more with happy chatter and last-minute preparations.

Most of the fete stalls circled the Moon Chestnut tree. There, Alex gave her leaf collage to the two grey mice who were running the raffle stall. She'd met Mo and May before – they'd kindly given the owls hot nettle milk to help them sleep when they'd stayed the night in Blossom Wood.

May assured Alex the collage was perfect. "In fact, I think we'll make this the special prize!" she squeaked as she stood next to a wooden table piled with acorn vases, moss-weave blankets, feather

scarves and other raffle donations. "I hope I win it," May added. "It would look wonderful in our little home and go so well with my sycamore-seed cushions, wouldn't it, Mo?"

Her husband nodded and grinned.

Meanwhile, Ruby the rabbit had called Eva over to her stall. It was decorated with a banner that read "Blossom Wood Bake Competition". Ruby admired Eva's rose-petal necklaces. "Oh my, they're stunning. Did you make them yourself? You're such a clever thing! What are you going to do with them?"

"I'm not sure – but I wanted to donate them to the fete somehow. Would you like them?"

Ruby beamed, revealing her long white teeth. "Oh, yes, please – they'd make perfect prizes for the competition!"

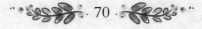

Billy, one of Ruby's children, poked his head up above the table. "Oh, wow, it's an owl! Can we play together today?"

Eva smiled. Ruby's son always seemed to be in awe of her, Alex and Katie. "I'm sure we can – once everything is ready." An idea popped into Eva's head, and she turned to Ruby. "Actually, can I borrow Billy for a moment? There's something I think he could help with. If you're happy to give us owls a hand, Billy?"

In answer, Billy leapt over the stall and landed right beside Eva. "Yes, please, I'd LOVE to!"

"And it'll help make sure he doesn't eat all the cakes!" chuckled Ruby.

Eva led Billy to a shady area where Katie had hammered a long log upright into the ground. She hovered in the air, tying each of her mum's ribbons round

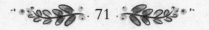

the top, while Alex hopped about on the ground below, checking they didn't get tangled.

"Hi, Billy," Alex said in her little voice when she spotted him. "Oh, you'd be great at maypole dancing! Would you like to try?"

Billy nodded his fluffy grey head so madly, Alex thought it might fall off. "YES, PLEASE!"

Eva winked at Alex. "That's exactly what I thought!"

Katie called down from above. "Billy, perhaps you could find some of your furry friends to join in too!"

It turned out to be a wonderful idea. First Bobby, still surrounded by Sara's young fawns, announced that the fete was open. Then the maypole dancing began. Animals, birds, insects and other creatures

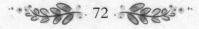

crowded around to watch young bunnies, squirrels and mice weave rainbow patterns around the pole. Katie had asked Charles if he could help with the music, and he'd organized a choir to tweet beautiful songs as the animals danced. Alex joined in with the dancing, which was huge fun – she was lucky to be just small enough to do it without getting caught up in the ribbons!

While everyone skipped around, enjoying the fete, Ruby asked Eva if she might like to judge the baking competition, since she'd been so kind as to donate the prizes.

"Oh, yes, I'd love to," Eva twittered. "Do you think my friends could help too?"

"Of course!" Ruby grinned her toothy smile and Eva, Katie and Alex were soon munching cake after cake.

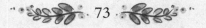 73

First came a honey tart with honeycomb icing. Alex could guess who'd made that – a bee! Next there were strawberry and vanilla cupcakes, then an apple gâteau, a hazelnut-and-treacle sponge and a lemon loaf with custard topping. Lastly, they ate blueberry profiteroles with walnut sprinkles. The cakes were all so delicious, the three best friends couldn't decide which was the best – but then Eva realized something: there were six cakes and six necklaces, so *everyone* could win! The creatures who'd made the cakes – a bee, a beaver, an otter, a squirrel, a fox and a rabbit – adored the necklaces, and wore them proudly for the rest of the fete.

Later, as the spring sunshine faded and the shadows lengthened over the wood, Mo and May announced the raffle. They

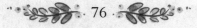

asked Bobby to pull numbered leaves
out of a basket to choose the winners.
The final prize was Alex's collage, and
everyone oohed and aahed as Bobby held
it up.

When May's number was read out, she
jumped in the air, squeaking even louder

than usual, "I won, I won, I won!"

"It's a great prize," said Katie, grinning at Alex. "Oh, look – there's Sara … and Flo!"

Sure enough, Sara was striding along the woodland path, with Flo trotting close behind her. Sara's other children rushed away from Bobby to leap around their mother and sister. Sara cuddled each of them in turn, before looking over to Katie, Alex and Eva. "I want to say thank you again for saving Flo. She's so little, and you did an amazing job to find her. To think – she hasn't even been blessed at the Moon Chestnut yet!"

"You could do it today!" Katie blurted out before she had time to think – and then felt her cheeks burn and hoped she hadn't sounded too bossy.

Sara swung her head down to Flo, then

back up to the owls, smiling. "What a perfect idea! Is everyone OK with that? I wouldn't want to disrupt the fete."

Bobby lumbered over and put a leathery paw on Sara's hoof. "I think we'd all agree it'd be a magical end to a most magical fete."

So that was settled. Sara led Flo to the hollow at the base of the Moon Chestnut tree, while the woodlanders surrounded it in a circle at least ten creatures deep. But although everyone was eager to see the blessing ceremony, they were all very considerate, letting the tiny insects stand at the front, with the small creatures behind them and taller animals at the back. The birds and butterflies flew in the air above – including Katie, Alex and Eva.

"I bring my daughter, Flo, to be blessed," Sara began in her glossy voice

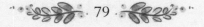

as she looked up at the towering Moon Chestnut tree. "May she live a long and happy life..." Then the deer moved her gaze down, scanning the crowd.

What's she looking for? Alex wondered, then bobbed her head in surprise when she realized Sara was staring straight at her.

"Alex, Katie and Eva, would you be Woodmothers to Flo?" Sara asked. "I haven't asked anyone yet, but I think she will need them, since she's already shown she's a rather adventurous deer!"

The three best friends didn't know what to say. *I haven't got a clue what a Woodmother is!* Katie thought. She didn't want to make a promise she couldn't keep.

Bobby came to the rescue. "Owls," he called up from the ground, "being a

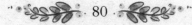

Woodmother or Woodfather means you are a special friend to the blessed creature and agree to give her advice and support as she grows up."

Eva swivelled her heart-shaped face towards her friends. "That sounds like something we can do!"

Katie gave a giant beam. "Yes, it does!"

"I'd love to be Flo's Woodmother!" Alex twittered.

They zoomed down to the hollow, feeling everyone's eyes on them. They stood in front of Sara and Flo, holding wingtips.

"Woodmothers, will you promise to help Flo in times of trouble, to give her advice and your love?" Sara asked.

They looked at the deer solemnly. "We promise," they chorused.

The watching animals cheered, hooted and clapped as Flo broke away from her

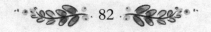

mum and hugged each of the owls
in turn.

As Eva cuddled the baby fawn, feeling
Flo's smooth fur on her feathery cheek,
she decided this might have been their
most magical day in Blossom Wood so far.
She hoped there would be many, many
more to come!

Did You Know?

❀ Squirrels really do use their tails for shelter when it's raining. The next time you're in a park and it's raining, see if you can spot one!

❀ It's true that deer like to swim — though not many people know that!

❀ Badgers live in setts, which are made up of tunnels and rooms under the ground. From the outside, you can usually see two or three large holes in mounds of soil. Have you ever seen one?

❀ Worms need to keep their skin wet to survive — which is why they appear above ground when it rains!

Look out for more

The Owls of
Blossom Wood

adventures!

The Owls of
Blossom Wood
A Magical Beginning

Catherine Coe

The Owls of Blossom Wood

To the Rescue

❧ To the Rescue ❧

Catherine Coe

❀ Would you like more animal
fun and facts?

❀ Fancy flying across the treetops in
the Owls of Blossom Wood game?

❀ Want sneak peeks of other
books in the series?

Then check out the Owls of
Blossom Wood website at:

theowlsofblossomwood.com

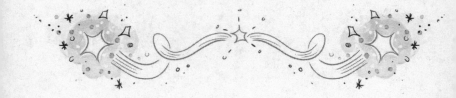